Anna Is Our Babysitter

By Brittany Candau

Illustrated by the Disney Storybook Art Team

 A GOLDEN BOOK • NEW YORK

Copyright © 2015 Disney Enterprises, Inc. All rights reserved. Published in the United States by Golden Books, an imprint of Random House Children's Books, a division of Random House LLC, 1745 Broadway, New York, NY 10019, and in Canada by Random House of Canada Limited, Toronto, Penguin Random House Companies, in conjunction with Disney Enterprises, Inc. Golden Books, A Golden Book, A Big Golden Book, the G colophon, and the distinctive gold spine are registered trademarks of Random House LLC.
randomhousekids.com
ISBN 978-0-7364-3405-8
Printed in the United States of America
10 9 8 7 6 5 4 3 2 1

$\mathcal{A}$nna shoved her feet into her boots. Her friends Kristoff and Sven would arrive any minute. They were all going to Troll Valley that evening to watch over the toddler trolls while the adult trolls went to their annual convention.

"Are you sure you don't need me to come?" Elsa asked. "My magic may come in handy."

"I think we've got it covered," Anna said, giving her sister a quick hug. "They're just babies. How hard could it be?"

Soon Anna, Kristoff, and Sven were off. They admired the beautiful glow of the setting sun as Kristoff told Anna stories about growing up with the sweet and silly trolls.

"I wonder if I should have brought games," Anna said. "Do trolls like games?"

"Oh, don't worry," Kristoff said. "They'll probably sleep the whole time. I bet we'll be relaxing by the fire all night, maybe eating some snacks."

He explained that Bulda, his adoptive mother, had a very strict bedtime for all the young trolls. Sven grunted in agreement.

As soon as they reached Troll Valley, they saw dozens of mossy rocks rolling toward them. Suddenly, the trolls appeared, and a chorus of greetings erupted.

"Kristoff! Sven! Anna! Welcome!"

"We missed you!"

"Anna, you're too skinny! Let me get you some mud pies," Bulda offered. Anna politely declined. Then Bulda thanked them for coming to troll-sit.

"It seems like just yesterday *you* were young enough to have a sitter, Kristoff," said Bulda.

"Remember when all he wanted to do was run naked through the valley?" Pabbie asked.

"Oh, really?" Anna asked, stifling a giggle. "You never mentioned that."

"Okay, that's enough stories for now," Kristoff said, groaning.

Bulda took Anna and Kristoff to the troll tots.

"If they get hungry, you can feed them smashed berries. And they may need a leaf change. But it's just about their bedtime, so they should be sleeping soon."

As the adult trolls headed off, Anna waved. "Have a great time! Everything is going to be . . ."

"... a disaster!"

Anna, Kristoff, and Sven had turned to see that the toddler trolls had escaped from their pen. They were running, climbing, and swinging all over the place.

"Oh ... no, no," Anna said, rushing to grab a few trolls who were climbing some boulders. "That's dangerous."

Kristoff ran over to the leaning tower of trolls that had just sprouted.

"All right, guys," Kristoff said, gently pulling the trolls off one another. "Let's settle down now."

But the more Kristoff and Anna tried to calm
the little trolls, the wilder they got.

"Maybe they're hungry!" Anna headed for the
basket of smashed berries. "Yummy!" she cooed.
But the trolls clearly felt they had better things to do.

"Maybe they need changing." Kristoff bravely peered into one of the trolls' leaf diapers. "Nope."

"Let's put them to bed," Anna suggested. "They've got to be tired by now."

But the young trolls were wide awake.

Suddenly, a cheery voice interrupted them.
"Hello, troll babies!"
It was their friend Olaf!

"Elsa sent me in case you needed some help," Olaf
explained, turning to the excited trolls. "Why, hi there.
Ha, ha! That tickles!"

"Boy, are we glad to see you," Kristoff said.

Anna ran to greet the snowman. But in her hurry she tripped and fell face-first into the basket of smashed berries! "Whoaaa!"

Kristoff rushed to her side. "Anna, are you okay?"

Anna lifted her head. Her face was covered in dripping purple goop!

The little trolls burst out laughing. They stampeded to her and lapped the berry juice from her cheeks.

Anna giggled. "Well, I guess that's one way to feed them."

After the trolls were done, they sat in a row, happy and full. Suddenly, a strange smell floated through the air. The trolls looked down at their leaves.

"Uh-oh," Kristoff said knowingly. "Olaf, you distract them."

Olaf happily told the little trolls stories about his favorite thing in the world: summer. Anna and Sven collected clean leaves while Kristoff changed the diapers. Soon everyone was dry and sweet-smelling once again.

"And now for my showstopping song about summer!" Olaf announced.

Anna noticed that the trolls were finally quiet. Some of them were even having trouble keeping their eyes open.

"Actually," she said to Olaf, "maybe Kristoff and Sven should sing a lullaby instead."

"Good thing I brought my lute," Kristoff replied. Anna and Olaf began to put the trolls to bed.

"Rock-a-bye, troll-ies, sleep time has come . . . ," Kristoff sang quietly.

By the time the adult trolls returned, the wee ones were sound asleep.

"Wow, great job," Bulda whispered.

"It was easy," Anna replied, elbowing Kristoff.

"Piece of mud pie," Kristoff added.

Bulda grinned. "You two will be great parents someday!"